For Jamie, my independent-minded piggie–M. P.

For Starr, with affection–H. C.

SIMON & SCHUSTER BOOKS FOR YOUNG READERS
An imprint of Simon & Schuster Children's Publishing Division
1230 Avenue of the Americas, New York, New York 10020
Text copyright © 2006 by Margie Palatini
Illustrations copyright © 2006 by Henry Cole
SIMON & SCHUSTER BOOKS FOR YOUNG READERS is a trademark of Simon & Schuster, Inc.
Book design by Einav Aviram
The text for this book is set in Oculus.
The illustrations for this book are rendered in watercolor, ink, and colored pencil.
Manufactured in China
2 4 6 8 10 9 7 5 3 1
Library of Congress Cataloging-in-Publication Data
Palatini, Margie.
Oink? / Margie Palatini ; illustrated by Henry Cole.
p. cm.
Summary: Frustrated because the pigs just lie around in the mud all day, the other animals on
the farm try to make them improve themselves.
ISBN-13: 978-0-689-86258-8
ISBN-10: 0-689-86258-X
[1. Pigs–Fiction. 2. Domestic animals–Fiction. 3. Humorous stories.]  I. Cole, Henry, 1955- ill. II. Title.
PZ7.P17550i 2006
[E]–dc22        2004006089

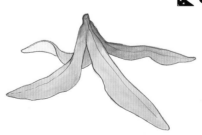

# OINK?

By Margie Palatini

Illustrated by Henry Cole

Simon & Schuster Books for Young Readers
New York  London  Toronto  Sydney

Thomas and Joseph were pigs.

They were sloppy.

They were lazy.

They were dirty.

And they were happy.

"Oink," said Thomas.

"Oink," agreed Joseph.

The pigs were very content.

Their neighbors were not as happy.

They were not so content.

"That place is a pig sty," clucked one hen to the other. "Disgraceful."

"Disgraceful," said the second hen with a knowing nod. "Untidy. Very untidy."

"Lazy is what they are," said the rabbit. "Not a green to be seen in all that pig slop. And a garden is just a hop away."

"And they stink!" added the duck. "My pond is downwind from those two."

"Disgraceful," said the first hen.

"Untidy," said the second.

"Lazy," said the rabbit.

"Pee-uw," said the duck.

Thomas and Joseph cared not one whit of what was whispered.

"Oink," said Thomas.

"Oink," agreed Joseph.

They were happy. They were content.

But their neighbors were not happy or content. They wanted something done about those pigs. And they wanted it done now.

"A dab or two of fresh paint and that place would not be so bad," said the first hen to the second.
"Not so bad," said the second to the first.

"A diet of fresh vegetables would do them a world of good," said the rabbit.

"A bath is what they need, if you ask me," concluded the duck.

So the neighbors made a plan.

The next day the hens, the rabbit, and the duck walked over to Thomas and Joseph.

They clucked. Tsked. Quacked. Quacked. Tsked. Clucked.

"Pardon me," said the first hen, "but you pigs look terribly sad."

"Sad," said the other neighbors. "Very sad."

"Oink?" said Thomas.

"Oink?" said Joseph.

"I myself am always happy being neat and tidy," said the hen.

"Happy. So happy," said the other chicken. "Perhaps if you paint your fence, you will be more cheerful."

Thomas and Joseph did not think painting a fence
would make them at all happier. They were cheerful now.
But the hens insisted. They gave the pigs two
big brushes and a bucket of white paint.

"Oink?" said Thomas.

"Oink?" said Joseph.

EXTERIOR
PAINT
EGGSHELL WHITE

"Dim-witted," whispered the first hen to the second. "They are very dumb pigs. I don't think they know what to do."

"Clueless," agreed the other. "We will just have to show them."

So they did.

Up. Down. Across. Up. Down. Across.

Thomas and Joseph tried.

This way. That way. *Sideways. Sideways.* That way. This way.

"Stop! Stop! You're making a mess," cried the first hen.

"A mess! A mess!" cried the other.

"They cannot paint," said the first hen to the second. "We can do it much better."

"Shoo! Shoo!" said the chickens to the pigs.

And the hens began painting the fence themselves.

Up. Down. Across. Up. Down. Across.

As the hens painted, the rabbit hopped over to Thomas and Joseph.

"I think some crisp lettuce and crunchy carrots would bring smiles to your faces."

"Oink?" said Thomas.

"Oink?" said Joseph.

The pigs were not at all certain a carrot could make them grin. But the rabbit insisted. She handed them each a basket and told them to go over to the garden and pick some vegetables for dinner.

Tramp. Stamp. Tramp. Stamp. *Yank. Yank.* Squash.

The rabbit was most distraught. The pigs were ruining the radishes. Destroying the cabbages.

"Scoot! Scoot!" she said to Thomas and Joseph. "Insufferable hogs."

She grabbed the baskets and began gathering the vegetables herself.

Hip. Hop. Hip. Hop. *Pull. Pull. Pull.*

And as the hens painted and the rabbit gathered, the duck waddled his way over to Thomas and Joseph.

"What you fellows need is a good long soak in some clear, clean water."

"Oink?" said Thomas.

"Oink?" said Joseph.

"Sure," said the duck. "Dig yourselves a little water hole right over here. Nothing beats a swim on a hot day."

Being fond of mud baths, Thomas and Joseph were not convinced a water hole would be all that refreshing. But the duck insisted. He brought out a shovel and showed them how it was done.

Dig. Lift. Dump.

Dig. Lift. Dump.

Thomas and Joseph took a turn.

They couldn't dig. They couldn't lift. They didn't dump.

"Move it! Clear out! Scram!" declared the duck.

He grabbed the shovel and began digging the hole himself.

Dig. Lift. Dump. Dig. Lift. Dump.

Up. Down. Across. Up. Down. Across.

Hip. Hop. Hip. Hop. *Pull. Pull. Pull.*

The hens, the rabbit, and the duck worked all day.

"I'm exhausted," sighed the hen, dropping the brush.

"Exhausted. Exhausted," said the second, dropping the bucket.

"Don't have a hip or a hop left in me," agreed the rabbit.

"I'm completely pooped," said the duck, dragging the last pail of water to the hole.

But—they were happy. They were content.

The fence was painted. The vegetables were picked. And the hole was dug and filled with clear, clean water. The four admired their work.

"Those pigs could not have done it without us," clucked the hens. "They don't know the first thing about painting a fence."

"Couldn't pick one leaf of lettuce without me," giggled the rabbit.

"Never even figured out how to use a shovel," snickered the duck.

The four began to laugh. And laugh. And laugh. And laugh.

And then they stopped laughing.

They looked at Thomas and Joseph.

Crunch. Munch.

Splish. Splash.

Chuckle. Chuckle.

"You know," said the hen. "I don't think they were as dumb as we thought they were."

"Not so dumb," said the other hen.

"Not so dumb at all," said the rabbit.

"Maybe," said the duck. "But I still say those two are a couple of big stinkers."

"Oink," said Thomas.

"Oink," agreed Joseph.